The Secret Diary of

Apple White

The Secret Diary of

Apple White

by *Heather Alexander*

LB

LITTLE, BROWN AND COMPANY
New York Boston

Little, Brown and Company
Hachette Book Group
1290 Avenue of the Americas, New York, NY 10104
Visit us at lb-kids.com
everafterhigh.com

First Edition: May 2017

Little, Brown and Company is a division of Hachette Book Group, Inc.
The Little, Brown name and logo are trademarks of Hachette Book Group, Inc.

The publisher is not responsible for websites (or their content) that are not owned by the publisher.

Library of Congress Control Number 2016959724

ISBNs: 978-0-316-46499-4 (hardcover), 978-0-316-46498-7 (ebook)

Printed in the United States of America

LSC-C

10 9 8 7 6 5 4 3 2 1

For Goldi, our princess

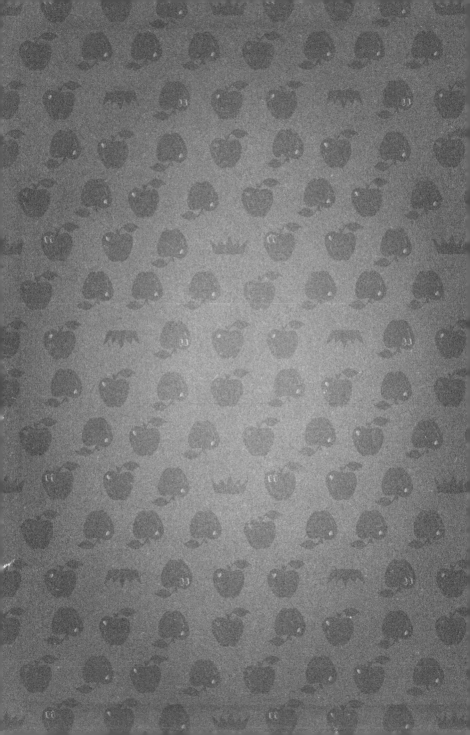

Diary Entry

This morning started like all mornings at Ever After High. The bluebirds on my windowsill chirped my favorite wake-up melody. The sun glinted through the white ruffled curtains, casting a happy glow on my canopy bed. I sat up and called out to my best friend forever after (who just so happens to be my roommate!) to wake her up.

Raven Queen grumbled, then buried her head under her purple comforter. Raven's not a morning person like I am, but that's okay. You and your BFFA don't have to have every little thing in common!

I stretched, got out of bed, slipped on my fluffy red robe, and tied the ribbon around my waist. Then I smoothed down my blond curls. They get a little bit poufy when I sleep.

Some people are surprised that the daughter of Snow White and the daughter of the Evil Queen are roomies. It was all my idea. We're part of the same fairytale, so I figured, why not get to know each other better by living together? And it was a spelltacular idea because now we're BFFAs. I like to think that I bring some sunshine to Raven's life. At least, I try to. A good leader should always make everyone's day brighter, and I want to be a good leader when I grow up.

I switched on the light, but don't worry—it didn't bother Raven, who was still enjoying a few more minutes of slumber at that point. (Raven can sleep through anything. She once slept through a parade of nine pipers piping down the hall!) I had a lot of work to do before breakfast. I had to put together the most hexcellent outfit for the school dance tonight.

I've worked really hard to make sure tonight's dance is hextra special. I'm on the School Activities Committee—I try to be on as many committees that bring happiness to the students as I can—and we vote on a theme for every dance, and I'm so hexcited that they liked my theme this time! I'm sure this is going to be the most spelltacular dance ever after!

Everyone on the committee helped decorate the Grimmnasium yeslerday, hexcept for Duchess Swan. She refused because her theme (Feathered Friends) wasn't chosen. That made me fairy sad, but I understand why she would be upset. Duchess put a lot of work into her theme, too. But still...

The school dance is not about one person or about winning and losing. It's about fun and being together! I wish I could help Duchess see that.

So, Diary, I bet you're wondering what my theme is. Drumroll, please...

My theme is the Enchanted Forest! Fableous, right? I can't wait to see it all come to life tonight!

Here's how we decorated: We lined the Grimmnasium with enormous paper trees with fuzzy felt leaves. Woven bird's nests filled with chocolate eggs were tucked into the branches. Garlands of tissue-paper flowers and tiny white lights, blinking like fireflies at dusk, crossed the ceiling. Chairs carved from tree stumps and little café tables decorated to look like giant red-and-white mushrooms surrounded the dance floor. The climbing ropes were fashioned into adorable swings. Shiny red apples waited in bins for bobbing contests, and bouquets of caramel apples sat on each table.

It was late when we finished transforming the Grimmnasium. We shut the door and hung a sign that said: ENCHANTED FOREST—do not enter until party time!

Now everything is ready, hexcept I don't know what to wear. I'm royally desperate to find just the right outfit. It has to say "enchanted forest" and have that special WOW factor.

I found a few options in my closet. Will you help me choose?

- a red dress with a layered skirt that fans out like the petals of a rose
- a shiny white skirt embroidered with blue butterflies
- a dress with cap sleeves in forest-green raw silk

I've already tried on each outfit and twirled around in front of the mirror, but I still can't decide! They are all so hexcellent. Which should I wear?

I would ask Raven for her opinion, but she just left with Madeline Hatter for breakfast. You know Maddie, Diary. Her dad is the Mad Hatter from Wonderland. When Maddie entered our room and saw my dresses and skirts flung around, she was fairy hexcited that everything was all topsy-turvy. Being from Wonderland, Maddie loves chaos. She's also not used to seeing our room looking like that. I'm usually fairy neat…hexcept when I am in the middle of an <u>Epic Fashion Crisis</u>.

Before Raven left for breakfast, she surveyed the tornado of clothes and offered to help me clean. Isn't she a great friend? But I couldn't tidy anything up until I found just the right dress, so I told Maddie and Raven to go without me. I promised I'd be right behind them, but here I am—almost an hour later—and I still have no idea what to wear tonight. Hexcept now my stomach is grumbling. I need to figure out this dress thing fast, or I'll miss breakfast—and a hungry princess is not a happy princess!

Charm you later!
Apple White

Chapter 1

Kitty Cheshire lay on her stomach on Lizzie Hearts's bed and lazily filed her pointy purple nails. She arched her back and yawned, although she'd woken up only a short time ago. Was it too early for a catnap?

Lizzie stood in front of her mirror, trying to balance her gold crown on her long black-and-red hair that was tied into a heart-shaped bump. The glittery crown slid to the left. Then to the right.

"You're taking *fur*-ever," purred Kitty.

"Off with my head!" cried Lizzie in frustration. "I am in need of a new hairstyle."

"Or a new accessory," offered Kitty. "Maybe a headband or a barrette?"

"Honest to nonsense," Lizzie huffed, finally setting the crown in place. "Queens-in-training wear crowns, not barrettes. The crown sends a message."

Lizzie was the daughter of the Queen of Hearts. She, Maddie, and Kitty, whose mother was the Cheshire Cat, had come to Ever After High from Wonderland.

"Message received." Kitty sat up and stretched. "Where's Faybelle? We'll miss breakfast if she doesn't come soon. I could really use a glass of warm milk."

"Here I am!" Faybelle Thorn flung open the door and scanned the small room. "Where's your roommate?"

"Duchess already went to breakfast," said Lizzie. "She was in a *fowl* mood this morning."

"Tell us something new," quipped Kitty.

Duchess, daughter of the Swan Queen, was never really in a good mood. Those in the know knew that it was because she hailed from a lesser-known fairytale that didn't end in a Happily Ever After. However, Lizzie knew today's particular bad mood stemmed from Apple's dance theme being chosen instead of Duchess's. But Lizzie never let Duchess's moodiness bother her.

"I did the spell," Faybelle announced with a sly grin.

"Did it work?" Lizzie asked.

"You're talking to the daughter of the Dark Fairy. Of course it worked." Faybelle fluttered her iridescent wings for dramatic effect. "I conjured two hundred little white mice and stashed them in a storage room."

"Oh, *mice*," Kitty said with a mischievous smile.

Faybelle rolled her eyes. "They're not for you to play with, Kitty. You know we need them for our prank."

The girls had been planning their big prank for weeks, and it was finally time to pull it off. Lizzie, however, was having last-minute jitters.

"Maybe it's too much," Lizzie said, bitting her cherry-glossed lip nervously.

"It's only a prank," said Kitty. "You know Mr. Badwolf will have to give us hextra credit if we pull it off. Just think how much chaos it will cause when we release the mice in the Castleteria! It's harmless but brilliant—the perfect prank!"

Lizzie paced back and forth. Her grade in Mr. Badwolf's General Villainy class definitely needed a boost. If her mother saw it now, heads would roll. She narrowed her eyes at Faybelle and Kitty. "I need the hextra credit, but you two don't. What's in it for you?"

"Hexcitement." Kitty yawned. "It's time to spice things up around here."

"Do I need a reason to cause trouble?" Faybelle arched her eyebrows. "Don't worry, Lizzie. We'll be hextra careful. I've been in trouble too many times with Headmaster Grimm this year. This isn't the sort of thing that'll get us in trouble. Like Kitty said, it's a harmless prank, but it will cause just enough chaos that Mr. Badwolf will be impressed."

"Fine," agreed Lizzie. She reasoned that Kitty knew how to stay out of sight, and Faybelle wouldn't put them at risk if she was already on thin ice with Headmaster Grimm. Besides, what was the worst that could happen with a few little mice?

Faybelle showed them to the storage closet. They hurried inside and carefully closed the door. Faybelle switched on the fluorescent light, revealing a large space lined with shelves that stored pencils and quills, hextbooks, and parchment scrolls. In the center of the floor sat four big metal cages, each filled with fifty tiny white mice.

"Oh cards! They're awfully cute," cried Lizzie. Their pink noses twitched and their whiskers wiggled. "Why did you conjure so many?"

"Go, go, go *big*! Or go, go, go *home*!" cheered Faybelle.

"But how are we getting them into the Castleteria? We can't just march down the hall with cages of mice," Lizzie pointed out.

"Obviously not." Faybelle focused her gaze on the cages. "I have that all figured out as well." She took a breath and started to cheer:

> *Give us a one, two, three!*
> *Give us a bling, bling, bling!*
> *We've got this in the bag!*
> *Go team!*

Faybelle was hexcellent at magic, but her spell-casting power was even stronger when she cheerhexed.

Instantly, three of the cages transformed into large bedazzled purses. One was red, one was teal, and one was purple. They all had mesh bottoms, so the mice could move around without being seen from the outside.

"The *purr*-fect accessory," said Kitty, lifting the glittery purple bag and taking a peek inside. The mice looked fairy content. "What about them?" Kitty pointed to the mice in the one cage still on the closet floor.

"*Hmmm...*" Faybelle fluttered her wings as she thought. "We'll come back for them. It'll look suspicious if one of us has two purses. I mean, who does *that*?"

"Good point." Kitty patted her purse. "So we just walk into the Castleteria, open our purses, and let the mice run wild?"

"Hexactly!" Faybelle bounced with anticipation in her lace-up boots.

"Wait a spell!" Lizzie cried. "Are we sure the Pied Piper won't be at breakfast? He can have the mice cleared out in no time, and what fun would that be?"

Faybelle sighed. "I thought of that, too, of course. But we're all set. He's out of town this week for a muse-ic conference. I'm telling you—I've thought of *everything*."

"Okay, let's do this." Kitty opened the closet door, checked the hallway, and crept out. Lizzie and Faybelle followed.

They hadn't gotten far before they heard heavy footsteps approaching.

"Girls!" Mrs. Trollworth called as she turned the corner.

"Act natural," Faybelle whispered. She smiled at Headmaster Grimm's trusty assistant. "Good morning, Mrs. Trollworth."

"Why aren't you in the Castleteria?" She adjusted her pink, pointy-tipped glasses to peer at each of them. "You're late for breakfast."

"We were just on our way to the Castleteria now," Kitty replied.

Mrs. Trollworth narrowed her eyes and stared at the girls suspiciously. Then she sniffed the air. For a moment, they were sure they were caught. But then Mrs. Trollworth cleared her throat and muttered, "I suddenly have the strangest craving for cheddar cheese soup. I wonder if I can find that old recipe my grand-mother used to make....Off you go, then."

"Thank you," Faybelle said quickly. Then she grabbed Lizzie's and Kitty's sleeves and hurried them away before Mrs. Trollworth became any more suspicious!

"Close call," said Kitty.

Faybelle pulled open the Castleteria doors and grinned at her friends. "Time for mice mayhem!"

Diary Entry

You'll never guess what I found today,
Diary.

A storage closet full of mice! Lots and
lots of mice!

I admit, Diary, that's not really what I
hexpected to happen when I left my room
this morning, but that's just what _did_ happen!

Back in my room, I narrowed down my
fashion choices to two dresses. I figured

I'd just ask Raven later which one she liked better. After all, what are best friends for? Besides, I didn't want to miss breakfast. A healthy breakfast is the <u>most</u> important meal of the day, especially when your day is as busy as mine!

I was skipping to the Castleteria when I heard the most curious sound. <u>Squeak. Squeak. Squeak.</u>

I stopped to listen. Mrs. Trollworth's gravelly voice came from somewhere down the hall, but it wasn't her. I followed the noise to a door I'd never noticed before. I knocked. No one answered. I knocked again. The only response was more <u>squeaks</u>, louder this time and sad-sounding.

Something needed my help!

I tried the knob, and the door swung open. I flicked on the light, and guess what I found! Oh...right. I told you already. I found mice! The cutest white mice huddled in a cage.

What were they doing here? I looked around. The closet stored classroom supplies. Why in Ever After would mice be here among the supplies?

I wiggled my fingers through the bars of the cage, petting the mice on their cute little pink noses. Now that I'd found them, I couldn't just leave them in a dark closet. I spread out my skirt and sat on the linoleum floor.

The mice looked at me with their little black eyes. They looked like they needed some playtime, so what else could I do? I unlatched the cage, and they happily scampered up my arms and across my ankles. Their tiny toes tickled!

But after all that playing, they really worked up an appetite! I needed to get them a snack, so I put them back in the cage—just for a few minutes, until I could return! I was sure that the line at the Castleteria would be much too long, so I decided to run to my room to grab one of my emergency snacks. And when I spotted you on my desk, Diary, I just needed to tell you all about my new mousy friends! They are just the cutest little snuggle bugs!

In fact, I think I'll take you with me, Diary. I wonder what they'll be up to when we get back to the storage closet!

Charm you later!
Apple White

Chapter 2

Faybelle, Kitty, and Lizzie watched the mice sprint into the Castleteria faster than Jack and Jill tumbled down the hill. For a moment, only a blur of white was visible— and then shrieks filled the air. Lizzie blinked in surprise, never hexpecting the prank to work so quickly.

A sly grin spread across Kitty's face. "They found the food," she whispered.

The mice leaped from the floor onto the tables. They danced in puddles of fairyberry jam. They jumped into the gooey filling of pixie pies. Their tiny feet left footprints in the frosting on thronecakes. One mouse tried to crawl through a glazed royalberry doughnut, and now waddled about with the pastry wrapped around its belly like an inner tube.

A group of mice bypassed the tables and made for the kitchen. Two mice seesawed on a big serving ladle. Others surfed across the floor on ogremeal cookies. Hagatha, the lunch lady, cried out as a mouse became tangled in the hairnet covering her gray beehive hairdo.

However, her cries were no match for Holly O'Hair's wails. Mice climbed her long braided auburn tresses to nibble the berries that crowned her head.

Faybelle nudged Kitty. "Check out Daring and Briar."

Daring Charming and Briar Beauty stood

on their chairs; Briar cringed at the sight of the mice while Daring let out high-pitched shrieks. They pointed in horror at a mouse doing the backstroke in a bowl of cereal. Raven gently plucked out the mouse by the base of its tail out of the milk, causing Daring to yelp even louder.

Under the same table, Maddie sat cross-legged, hosting a tiny tea party for her rodent friends. She served charmomile tea and tea-cakes cut into mouse-size bits. "The dormice in Wonderland thought berry tea was tear-rific," she told them.

"Daring, please stop screaming," Rosabella Beauty pleaded. "Ashlynn and I can't help if the mice can't hear us."

At the base of the large tree that grew in the center of the Castleteria, Ashlynn Ella and Rosabella fed thronecake crumbs to a group of mice who had gathered around them. Rosabella was always there to care for animals, big and small. And Ashlynn could communicate with animals, since she was the daughter of Cinderella. Together, they tried their best to calm the mice, but it wasn't easy. The Castleteria was far, far away from calm.

"Whoa!" cried Dexter Charming as he slipped on a spilled hocus latte. His feet flew out from under him, sending the bowl of porridge that he'd been carrying into the air. The porridge landed with a *splat* on Sparrow Hood's green fedora.

"That's totally not cool, man!" Sparrow wiped thick globs of porridge from his forehead. Then Sparrow flung his fried egg like a Frisbee in Dexter's direction. The egg missed Dexter, landing instead on Hunter Huntsman's face. For a moment, Hunter froze, unable to see through the rubbery yolk.

"Now it's on, Sparrow," he called, tossing the egg to the floor. He tucked a mouse down the back of Sparrow's studded leather jacket. Sparrow shimmied awkwardly as the mouse ran down his spine, into his pants, and right into his boot. He ripped off his shoe, and the mouse finally scampered out.

"New dance for the Merry Men?" Tucker teased Sparrow. Tucker and Sparrow were in the same rock band.

But Sparrow was too busy scooping the porridge from his hat to throw at Hunter. The Castleteria had erupted into an epic food fight—complete with one hundred and fifty mice!

"Clydesdale, come back! Don't play with them!" Farrah Goodfairy, the daughter of the

Fairy Godmother, chased after her pet mouse who'd joined the fray. She knocked over a pitcher of ice water, sending the ice cubes skittering across the floor.

"We deserve *hextra* hextra credit." Faybelle rubbed her hands together with glee.

Lizzie pointed to the door. "Uh-oh! Here comes trouble."

Headmaster Grimm stormed in, his blue coat flapping. His green eyes widened as he stared, momentarily speechless, at the royal mess and the mice running wild. Then he found his voice. "Everyone, halt!"

"Time to go," Faybelle whispered to Kitty and Lizzie.

All the students stopped throwing food, but the mice kept munching. Breadcrumbs covered every surface.

"What is the meaning of this?" hexclaimed Headmaster Grimm as he scanned the Castleteria for the troublemakers. "Who's responsible?"

Everyone shrugged, trying to recall who had thrown the first egg or spilled the first glass of milk.

"Honestly, Headmaster Grimm, it was the mice," piped up Cedar Wood, the daughter of Pinocchio. "They came running in and ate our food and then things got a little wild."

Headmaster Grimm stroked his mustache. Cedar always told the truth. "The mice had to come from somewhere. Who brought them in here?"

He was met with more shrugs. One mouse ran up the clock, even though it was hours away from one o'clock.

"I could ask them for you, Headmaster

Grimm," Ashlynn offered. The Castleteria grew silent as Ashlynn whispered with an important-looking mouse.

"He says three girls brought them here," she finally announced.

"Which three girls?" Headmaster Grimm huffed.

Ashlynn had the mouse climb into the palm of her hand. Gently, she raised her arm above her head so he could view all the students. The mouse spoke into Ashlynn's ear.

"He says the three girls aren't here," she reported.

"How can that be? Students shouldn't be missing breakfast. No one move until Madam Baba Yaga deals with the mice," grumbled Headmaster Grimm. "I'm going to check the halls."

Baba Yaga floated into the Castleteria on

her magic pillow. She waved her arms and chanted a spell that made all the mice scurry into a corner. Mr. Badwolf guarded them while Baba Yaga conferred with the other teachers.

"Psst," Raven whispered under the table to Maddie. "Where's Apple?"

Maddie peered out. "I don't see her."

"She must still be in our room trying to choose an outfit," said Raven.

Raven and Maddie shared a concerned look. This wasn't the best morning for Apple to start skipping breakfast.

Diary Entry

Mice update:

☑ Bellies full. That emergency
  granola bar I keep in my room
  really did the trick! I broke it
  up and gave them all itty-bitty
  pieces. (Luckily, I also had an
  apple in my room...at the rate

I'm going, I might not make it to breakfast after all!)

☑ Happy. I sang their fairy favorite song four times. It goes: <u>I think mice are nice.</u> <u>Oh, I think mice are nice!</u> <u>So fairy, fairy nice!</u>

☑ ~~Nap~~ time. ~~After~~ all that fun, eating, and singing, they snuggled against me and drifted off to dreamland.

Every creature—big and small—is spelltacular, but these little guys are the fairest of them all.

Good thing you're with me, Diary. You always help me work through the stickiest problems. I could never-ever-after find it in my heart to put the mice back in their cage and imprison them for who knows how long! All creatures deserve to be free. But I can't open the door and let them roam the halls, either. They'd be stepped on, for sure, not to mention all the chaos they could cause.

So what is a princess to do with fifty mice?

The answer is royally obvious: They could live in my room until their owner comes back. I'd feed them and keep them safe. Hexcept, what would Raven think? We are roomies after all. Would she want to adopt them, too? Most woodland creatures are scared of her because of the whole Evil Queen connection, even though Raven totally isn't like her mom.

I need a plan to persuade her.

Maybe I could teach the mice to clean Raven's side of the room.

Or they could bring her thronecakes whenever-after she wanted.

I'm sure I'll find a way.

I promise to keep you safe, cute little sleeping mice!

Hold on—was that someone outside the door?

Wait a spell, Diary...someone is coming! I think the owner of the mice must be returning. Maybe I won't miss breakfast ever after all!

Charm you later!
Apple White

Chapter 3

"Faybelle?" Apple scrambled to stand and smooth her flouncy skirt as fifty mice awoke with a start. "What are you doing here?"

"What are *you* doing here?" Faybelle shot back.

"Is that Lizzie? And Kitty?" Apple was sure she spotted Lizzie and Kitty lurking in the shadows behind Faybelle.

"You didn't answer me." Faybelle crossed her arms. "And why are the mice running free?"

Apple's mind whirred, trying to fit all

the pieces together. Did the mice belong to Faybelle?

"I found them...I mean, they were sad, so I—Wait, you know about the mice?" Apple fumbled for a response. In the distance, she heard shouting and footsteps.

"Uh-oh, I'm out of here. Spell you later," Kitty said before disappearing until just her wide smile lingered, which then vanished along with the rest of her. Kitty had the ability to make herself invisible.

"Girls!" Headmaster Grimm's voice echoed down the hall. His footsteps grew closer and closer.

Lizzie stepped into the closet. "Faybelle, we need to go. *Now!*"

Faybelle moved to shut the door, when a mouse scurried out. Then another. And another.

"Oh no!" Apple lunged forward. She scooped

up two mice, just as Headmaster Grimm appeared in the doorway. Mice scampered around his feet. One grabbed his shoelace and gave it a tug.

"What in Ever After is going on in here?" he shouted.

"We found Apple playing with the mice in this closet," Faybelle replied quickly.

"Apple?" The headmaster looked perplexed. Apple White—the co-president of the Royal Student Council!—was standing in a closet surrounded by mice. Her red book bag lay on the floor, and next to it, mice licked the crumbs off a granola bar wrapper. Several more slept on her red quilted jacket.

"Are these your mice?" he asked Apple.

"Well…maybe…you could say that," Apple said. "They're kind of mine. I'm taking care of them right now, but I only just…"

Faybelle pointed to Apple. "See? It was all her idea. She did it."

"Wait a spell. What was my idea?" Apple was confused. "Do you mean taking them out of the cage?"

"So *you* let the mice out?" Headmaster Grimm asked.

"Well, yes, because they were trapped," Apple hexplained. She had no idea what had gone on in the Castleteria. "They are much happier out of the cage," she added.

"Happy?" the headmaster sputtered, stepping out of the doorway. "Do you think that mess makes *me* happy?"

"What are—?" Before Apple could finish, the first period bell rang. The loud noise startled the mice, and they rushed through the open doorway and into the hallway.

Students streamed out of the Castleteria.

The halls would be packed—Apple had to round up the mice before the students started rushing through the hallway. Apple knew that dozens of mice and hundreds of students would spell disaster!

"Come back!" Apple shouted as she hurried past Headmaster Grimm, Faybelle, and Lizzie. She raced after the mice.

"Ms. White!" called Headmaster Grimm. "I'm not done speaking with you."

Apple knew she shouldn't disobey the headmaster. But she'd promised the mice she would keep them safe, and there was no safe space in the crowded hallway. She *had* to rescue the mice. It was the fairest thing of all to do.

"I'm sorry," Apple called over her shoulder as she ran after them. "Let me just get the mice and I'll be right back!"

"Apple White, are you ignoring the rules now?" Headmaster Grimm called after her in shock. Apple *never* broke the rules.

"Oh for Queen's sake! All the mice have escaped now," Lizzie cried as the last mouse scurried down the hall.

"What in Ever After are you two doing here?" Headmaster Grimm eyed Faybelle and Lizzie suspiciously. "Why aren't you at breakfast?"

"We *were* at breakfast. We left early to help find the culprit," said Faybelle. "I thought that perhaps my special skills in Villainy could be of assistance in figuring out who did this."

"So you have nothing to do with these mice?" he asked.

"Well—" began Lizzie. She kept trying to get a word in to defend Apple, or, at the fairy least, tell the truth.

But again, Faybelle cut her off. "Apple is

the one chasing them. Actions speak loudest, don't they?"

Headmaster Grimm let out a frustrated sigh, then stormed into the hallway after Apple.

Apple dodged Dexter and Hunter as she tried to keep the mice in sight. "Please, stop!" she cried.

The mice didn't stop. They ran hither and thither and all aquiver. Apple wished she could talk to animals the way Ashlynn could. She wished she could run as fast as Cerise Hood. She wished she'd worn sneakers instead of her cute patent-leather heeled shoes. She royally wished these mice would just slow down!

"Where are you going, Apple?" called Humphrey Dumpty from the low wall by the water fountain.

Apple didn't know the answer, but she

made sure to wave as she ran by. Even a high-speed mouse chase was no hexcuse to be rude.

"This is Blondie Lockes, reporting live at Ever After High." Blondie held up her Mirror-Phone, filming Apple's hallway sprint for her MirrorCast. "We are witnessing Apple White in action. Is she late for class? Trying out for Track and Shield? Being chased by a big, bad wolf? Oh!" At that moment, several mice scurried past. "Apple is running with rodents. Smile, Apple!"

Apple smiled for the camera, then frowned.

Where did all the mice go? She could no longer see them in the crowded hallway. She spotted crowns, fairy wings, billy goats, trolls, and princes—but no mice.

"Mouse!" Briar's high-pitched squeal vibrated

down the hall. Mr. Badwolf clapped his ears in pain.

Apple wove her way toward Briar, with Blondie following close behind. "Hexcuse me, please. Let me through, please. *Please!*"

"Oh, Apple, help! There are *mice* in the Grimmnasium." Briar held up her skirt and stood on tiptoes.

The DO NOT ENTER sign Apple had attached last night for the dance still hung on the Grimmnasium door, but now the door was slightly ajar. Familiar squeaking came from inside.

Oh curses! Apple's stomach dropped as she stepped into the Grimmnasium.

Mice were everywhere—ripping the tissue-paper flowers, popping the balloons, gnawing on the rope swings, knocking over the fake trees, eating the chocolate eggs, tangling the little twinkling lights, and splashing water as they bobbed with the apples. The committee's hard work had been destroyed in minutes.

"Please, don't do that!" Apple called to the mice.

Nothing could calm the mouse frenzy. They trailed sticky caramel footprints across the once-shiny floor now littered with shredded decorations. Strings of tangled lights crashed to the floor, and felt leaves were ripped from the branches.

"Ms. White! Hexplain yourself immediately!" Headmaster Grimm marched over to her. His face was red from running, and he struggled to catch his breath.

Apple stared at the mouse-made disaster. She didn't know why the mice had been in the closet or who'd put them there or why they had destroyed her beautiful Enchanted

Forest dance. She shook her head silently. Apple couldn't hexplain it.

"Report to my office. I will meet you there after I deal with the mice." He straightened his tie and smoothed his vest.

"Deal with the mice? How?" Apple knew the mice shouldn't be blamed. "They didn't mean to make a mess. They were just being mice."

"Baba Yaga will use magic to round up the mice and send them to the meadow to live Happily Ever After," he informed her. "They will be treated with the utmost respect and care."

After all, Headmaster Grimm was an animal lover, too.

Apple was pleased her mouse friends would have a nice place to live. The meadow was pretty when the spring flowers bloomed with silver bells and cockleshells. "Will you give them something delicious to eat, too?"

"Enough questions from you, Ms. White." He shook his head in dismay. "You are in heaps of trouble. To my office. Now!"

Diary Entry

Detention.

I have detention. Me! How can this be? I'm co-president of the Royal Student Council. I serve on several committees to make Ever After High the most spelltacular place it can be. I make things happy and good. I help my fellow students—I don't cause trouble.

What a fairy-fail!

And I still don't understand hexactly what happened.

I did what Headmaster Grimm said and went over to his office. When I got there, Mrs. Trollworth thought I was there to collect another award or help organize the school cleanup. That's how fairy strange it was for me to be in trouble! Of course, I told her the truth: Headmaster Grimm sent me there because I was in trouble. I had to repeat myself three times because she thought her built-up earwax was making her hear things. (Fairy gross, I know, but that's what she said!) But then she finally told me to go sit with the others.

And, Diary, "the others" were Kitty, Faybelle, and Lizzie. Faybelle told me that they orchestrated this whole prank to get hextra credit points for Mr. Badwolf's class! But even after all that, he ended up sending them to the headmaster's office anyway. I guess even General Villainy teachers have to draw the line somewhere.

I was relieved to see Lizzie there. We don't always see crown-to-crown in Kingdom Management class, but Lizzie is still fairy nice. I was sure she would help me sort things out with Headmaster Grimm.

Finally, Headmaster Grimm entered. He sat down in his chair behind his heavy oak desk, and we lined up in front. My knees trembled. Have I mentioned that

I've never been in trouble? I did not like this feeling at all.

Then he said, "Let's talk about why the three of you are here."

Three? I looked around and realized that Kitty had disappeared right before Headmaster Grimm had even noticed her. How tricky!

He told us that Mr. Badwolf informed him about "our" prank and that it had gone too far. It was more than a prank, he said. It was the destruction of school property. Students had been scared, and someone could have been injured. (Thank goodness no one was!) Food was wasted and contaminated.

I felt as if I'd started a book from the middle instead of the first page. Why was he talking about the Castleteria?

Then I found out: There was more than one batch of mice, and the first group made a mess in the Castleteria. Then the second batch of mice destroyed the Grimmnasium and all the dance decorations. Headmaster Grimm said he's heard from "a hexcellent source" that three girls did it. I gulped as I realized that with Kitty gone, I looked like the third accomplice!

I didn't want to get Kitty in trouble, but I had to defend myself! I protested that I wasn't even in the Castleteria. But Faybelle just kept saying that my not being there proved I was involved!

Lizzie tried to stand up for me and tell the truth, but Faybelle just talked over her. That girl is going to make a hexcellent Dark Fairy one day.

I'm not proud of this, but I got fairy frustrated and raised my voice and tried to talk louder than Faybelle. That made Faybelle get even louder, and then Lizzie got frustrated and started yelling, "Off with your heads!" and it got so bad that Headmaster Grimm slammed his hand down on his desk and boomed, "Enough!"

The headmaster told us that he was fairy disappointed in us for pulling the prank. I felt like he was hextra disappointed in me.

And then, Diary, he gave us detention.

We can't attend class today until the Castleteria and the Grimmnasium are cleaned and spotless.

He told Lizzie she couldn't order other students to help.

He told Faybelle she couldn't use any magic.

Then he looked right at me and told me not to get any help from woodland creatures. The three of us created the mess, he said, and the three of us would clean it all up.

I was fine with that, Diary. I felt responsible for the mess in the Grimmnasium, and I wanted to fix it and hang new decorations. I'm not afraid of hard work and a little elbow grease.

But he wasn't done.

He said that we might have released the mice and set the mayhem in motion, but our fellow students also took part. They threw food, misbehaved, and did not act in accordance with their fairytales. Therefore, he ruled that tonight's dance is canceled.

Canceled?

He has to be kidding. Right?

Charm you later,

Apple White

Chapter 4

Headmaster Grimm never kidded or teased or joked while at the helm of Ever After High. Parents sent him their precious children to mold into upstanding storybook characters, so they'd grow up to fulfill their destinies and do the kingdom proud. Dances were delightful little details that he could delete from the script. And now that the decorations were destroyed, it was easier to cancel the dance than have the students spend time making new ones.

He refused to change his mind.

Apple walked in a daze down the hallway toward the Castleteria, letting Faybelle and Lizzie go ahead of her. Bad news traveled faster than word of a lost glass slipper. The whispering started and grew louder. Students hexclaimed in amazement that Apple was responsible for the dance being canceled. They wondered if she had flipped her crown. They couldn't believe it.

Neither could Apple.

Apple knew she wasn't guilty in the same way Faybelle and the other girls were, but she did hold herself accountable. She had let the mice out of the closet, and they'd destroyed the lovely decorations in the Grimmnasium. Guilt churned around inside her like undigested apple seeds.

"How could you do something so selfish,

Apple White?" Duchess blocked her path. "Now the dance is canceled, and it's all your fault!"

"Wait a spell. It wasn't like that," Apple protested. "I really never meant for this to happen. I was more hexcited for the dance than anyone."

Duchess turned up her nose. "A likely story. I think you did it for attention. It's a publicity stunt."

"Why would I want detention attention?" asked Apple.

"With the dance canceled, you won't have to be embarrassed that your theme wasn't as good as mine, because no one will ever see yours." Duchess rested her hands on her hips. "Now you can *pretend* it would've been great."

Apple didn't want to argue with Duchess. What was the point? Her mind was made up. Surely, the other students would believe that Apple had never meant for any of this to happen.

Right?

Duchess turned to the crowd of students that had gathered behind her. "See? She doesn't deny it. Blondie broadcasted it all. Everyone saw Apple lead the mice to the Grimmnasium."

"I wasn't leading them," Apple protested. "It's not what it looked like."

"It *looks* like you took away our dance," Duchess declared.

Disappointed faces stared at Apple. The students weren't smiling like they always did when they saw her. Several students refused to even make eye contact with her. She had disappointed everyone.

Apple ran down the hall, past the Castleteria, and all the way back to her dorm, where she flung open the door to her room.

Diary Entry

Diary, this day has just been spelltacularly terrible. Duchess has helped turn most of the student body against me—but I can't even blame her. I've let everyone down! I was feeling so frustrated that I was tempted to climb into bed and pull the covers over my head, but that's not what I did. My mother always says no good comes from wallowing in self-pity. I've also heard her say that problems don't solve themselves. I'm taking her advice. Surely, there is something I can do to straighten things out.

Raven came charging into our room a few minutes after I got back, and she had Maddie and Rosabella with her. They were all concerned and wanted to make sure I was okay. I thanked my friends for their concern and told them I was fine.

Raven was _fuming_! She said, "You can't be fine. Headmaster Grimm was royally unfair."

My friends told me that they knew I didn't team up with Faybelle to scare everyone with a mess of mice and then destroy the dance. Raven said she knew me too well to believe this could possibly be my fault. I thanked her. It's so nice to have such a loyal friend.

Then it dawned on me that Raven hadn't asked to hear my hexplanation. Like Headmaster Grimm, she'd jumped to her own conclusion. So I told her hexactly what had happened from beginning to end. Raven was still pretty upset for me. She wanted me to tell the headmaster that Faybelle lied. But the thing is, Diary, I _did_ open the cage in the closet and let the mice out. The Grimmnasium mess was kind of my fault. And it was up to me to fix it.

All of a sudden, Diary, I knew what to do. I needed to handle this like a future queen—like my mom, Snow White. So I told my BFFAs that I, Apple White, needed to fix this whole mess. And to do that, I needed to sit alone, find my inner leader, and think, think, <u>THINK</u>!

After they each gave me a big hug and headed to the library to study, I thought about how my mom would handle this. She would probably consider everyone else's perspectives.

She'd say that even though Duchess's words stung, I shouldn't take what she said personally. Duchess was angry that her theme wasn't chosen, and like everyone else, she was upset the dance had been canceled. I can understand that. I just wish she could see that we were on the same side—that I want the dance, not because it was my theme, but because dances bring the students together. And they're fun. And we all get to wear the most fabulous dresses.

Then Mom would probably say that Faybelle only said I was involved in the prank because she's the daughter of the Dark Fairy. She likes to cause a little trouble—but I don't think she meant to get me into _too_ much trouble. Plus, I still feel fairy terrible about letting the mice escape...and ruining all the decorations. Helping clean up is the least I can do.

But, most important, I need to remember the other thing my mother always says: The great leaders focus on the BIG PICTURE. And the big picture here is the _dance_.

I need to get it un-canceled. Okay, Diary, what in Ever After should I do? Any ideas?

...

I've got it!

I am going to clean the Castleteria and the Grimmnasium fableously fast. Then I'm going to use my best negotiation skills and persuade Headmaster Grimm to reverse his decision. Oh! I can't wait to hext Raven, Maddie, and Briar that I have a plan!

I'm going to make what's done UNdone.

It's time to fix things.

Charm you later!

Apple White

Chapter 5

pple entered the Castleteria ready to clean. She wore a crisp white apron over her red gingham dress and white cleaning gloves that reached up to her elbows. Her golden curls were clipped into a loose bun. She carried a feather duster.

"Look who finally showed up," Faybelle snapped. She lazily picked eggshells off the floor and tossed them into a garbage bin. "So nice of you, Apple, to grace us with your royal presence."

Think big picture, Apple told herself. *It's about the dance.*

She smiled. "Sorry I'm late. What should I clean first?"

Mrs. Trollworth peered over the edge of her glossy magazine. The cover of *Ogre Life and Home* featured an ogre lounging by the side of a mud puddle while drinking a frosty glass of swamp juice. "Take your pick. There's enough mess to keep you girls busy for hours."

Lizzie chipped away at the icky, hardened porridge on the tables with a metal spatula. Apple reached for a sponge, dunked it in soapy water, and scrubbed alongside her.

Mrs. Trollworth burped several times, emitting a pungent odor that mixed poorly with the sour smell of spilled milk.

"Hexcuse me." She placed her magazine

on a chair and stood. "My belly doesn't take to sitting. You girls don't need me to watch over you, do you?" She didn't wait for an answer and waddled toward the door. "Keep at it. I'll check back."

As soon as she left, Faybelle abandoned her garbage bin and Lizzie tossed down her spatula. Faybelle sat on a clean chair and leaned back.

Apple kept scrubbing, but it seemed the work would never be done. She eyed the girls. How long of a break were they planning on taking?

Apple reached for a mop and pail. With the mop, she swished a little to the left. Then a little to the right. Then she spun around and dunked the mop back in the pail. Apple repeated this again and again until she got into a perfect rhythm. Mopping was actually pretty fun! In fact, Apple was enjoying herself so much that she let out a happy little laugh.

"I demand to know what's so funny!" yelled Lizzie. Lizzie could sound fairy stern, but in reality, she was much nicer than you'd hexpect the daughter of the Queen of Hearts to be.

"I was pretending the mop was a handsome prince," Apple hexplained. "It makes cleaning fun. There are more mops. We could have a dance-off!"

"Wait a spell." Faybelle waved Apple away. "Why would we clean? Trollworth took off."

"She's gone?" Kitty said as she suddenly materialized with a bottle of periwinkle nail polish. "Mani-curses, anyone?"

"Oh yes!" Faybelle fluttered her fingers.

"For the love of Wonderland! I only wear

red. Do you have scarlet or crimson polish?" Lizzie asked with a smile.

"No, no, no." Apple hurried over. "You can't clean if your nails are wet."

"Who said we were cleaning?" Faybelle challenged.

"If we can tidy everything up quickly, then we can ask Headmaster Grimm not to cancel the dance," Apple hexplained.

Kitty surveyed the Castleteria and yawned. "It's an awful lot of work."

"Not if we do it together. Think of how happy everyone will be if there's a dance tonight. We can divide and conquer the chores. Lizzie can sweep. Kitty can sponge. Faybelle can scrub. And I can mop. What do you say? Are we in this together?" Apple waited hexpectantly, her clear-blue eyes shining.

"I don't want to get into more trouble." Lizzie reached for the broom.

"Whatever-after," said Faybelle. She didn't reach for anything.

"I'll help after my nap." Kitty curled up on a table and closed her eyes.

At least I have Lizzie with me, Apple thought. She dipped the mop in the pail of soapy water.

A few minutes later, Apple decided to give Lizzie some helpful advice.

"Lizzie, it's better if you don't sweep the old orgemeal cookies where I'm mopping. It's getting all soggy. Why don't you sweep over there?" Apple directed cheerfully.

"Off with your mop-head! I'll sweep the floor with you!" Lizzie cried.

"I'm sorry. I was only trying to help," said Apple.

"Reverse!" Lizzie replied. She liked to give orders. "You sweep. I'll mop."

They switched jobs.

"Um, Lizzie ... you're splashing me," Apple said a few moments later, wiping droplets off her apron. "Maybe try using less water?"

Lizzie let the mop clatter to the floor. "Oh bother. I decree a leave of absence for this future queen."

Apple sighed with frustration. No one was listening to her. If she couldn't get them to clean maple syrup from a chair, how would she rule her subjects someday? What was happening to Apple's leadership skills?

I can tidy everything myself if I need to, Apple decided. Her mother had cooked, cleaned, and sewed for seven dwarves. Apple could certainly mop up some orange juice.

Apple stacked the dirty dishes in a bin. She hummed as she deposited the shredded napkins in the garbage can. She liked making everything beautiful.

Soon, she realized that her humming was the only sound in the quiet Castleteria.

Had the others left?

No. Faybelle was bent over her notebook, writing new cheers for the cheerhexing squad. She twirled her platinum-blond hair with one finger as she chanted the rhymes under her breath. Lizzie had built a tall castle with a turret and moat using her deck of cards. She balanced one card on top of another with complete concentration. Kitty napped peacefully, grinning as she dreamed. And Mrs. Trollworth still hadn't returned.

Apple waited for anger to rush over her, but it never came. With a shock, she realized she wasn't angry. They were each doing what they were good at and what they were destined to do. She couldn't change their stories.

The big hickory-dickory-dock-clock chimed twelve o'clock. Time was running out. If she wanted to clean the Grimmnasium, make new decorations for the dance, and plead her case to Headmaster Grimm, Apple realized she couldn't do it on her own.

Apple glanced again at the three girls. Persuading them to lend a hand would take a lot of time, and she didn't have time right now. Headmaster Grimm had called in a group of professionals to clean the kitchen. Apple needed professionals by her side, too.

She bit her lip. What should she do? They had been instructed not to use hextra help, and Apple always followed the rules.

She thought of all the students depressed

about the dance. She thought of the care that had gone into planning it.

This will not be the end of this storybook! Apple decided she would do whatever it took to get this dance back on story.

She whistled. High, then low. High, then low.

Silently, help arrived in the form of cute little woodland creatures.

Three raccoons wiped down the tables with their furry tails. Two rabbits wrapped towels around their feet and hopped about, shining the floor. Chipmunks tucked spilled food into their cheeks. Sparrows plucked up bits of trash with their beaks and flew it over to the garbage cans. A skunk sprayed a lilac scent to freshen the air, while a fawn licked the window with her pink tongue.

Apple helped them clean. *"This is the way we sweep the floor,"* she sang softly.

Faybelle stopped writing cheers. Lizzie knocked down her card castle. Kitty woke up. They stared in amazement at Apple's woodland cleanup crew.

"Am I seeing this right? Did Apple White just break a rule?" asked Faybelle.

"I didn't want to do it. Really, I didn't," Apple replied. "As a general rule, I don't like to break rules, but I gave it a lot of thought. So many others are affected by the dance being canceled. It's unfair of us not to consider their feelings. My mother always says a good ruler trusts her judgment. I decided that one small wrong would be okay to help make a big right." She waved in their direction. "I was on my own. I didn't have any other option to make everything end Happily Ever After."

The three girls said nothing. Faybelle avoided Apple's gaze. Kitty arched her back, and Lizzie flushed red. For the first time today, they felt ashamed.

"I'm heading to clean the Grimmnasium now." Apple walked out with the woodland creatures.

To her surprise, Faybelle, Lizzie, and Kitty stood and followed her.

Diary Entry

Surprise, surprise!

Our walk from the Castleteria to the Grimmnasium held _way_ more surprises than I hexpected!

The woodland creatures scurried ahead. Kitty lounged on top of the lockers, occasionally reappearing farther down the hallway. Faybelle shuffled behind me. Lizzie pulled out a croquet mallet and tapped a crumpled ball of paper down the hall as we walked.

The school was fairy quiet. Classes were in session. I was missing Crownculus, and I hoped that Humphrey would lend me his notes. I'm going to have a lot of makeup thronework to do.

I hesitated in front of the closed door leading to Headmaster Grimm's office.

I wondered aloud if we should tell Mrs. Trollworth we were moving on, but Faybelle said she'd only ruin our fun. Had I skipped a page, Diary?

Surprise #1: Faybelle thought we were having fun! Okay, then. Off we went.

After that, the three of us walked together. Kitty stayed on the ceiling. She has a thing for heights. Then the bell rang. Classroom doors opened, sending students streaming into the hall.

And, of course, Surprise #2: Duchess came storming down the hallway. She announced that she was going to talk to Headmaster Grimm about having the dance and doing it her way. She made sure to mention how my theme was so last chapter anyway.

Then Duchess spotted me. "Check out the merry maid. Yesterday, you were a queen-in-training. Today, you're scrubbing floors. The apple has fallen fairy far from the royal tree."

My mother taught me that if I don't have anything nice to say, I should speak with a smile. With Duchess, I smiled so hard, my cheeks hurt.

Suddenly, Duchess let out an unintentional honk, then dropped the folder she was carrying. Papers scattered everywhere! Then she blamed me for it so loudly that a big crowd of students gathered around.

Whatever-after was she talking about? I didn't do anything. I wasn't close enough to touch her.

And that, Diary, is when <u>Surprise #3</u> happened: Lizzie, Faybelle, and Kitty came to my defense!

Lizzie and Faybelle insisted that I hadn't done anything. Then Kitty

appeared right between Duchess and me.
She told Duchess to walk away if she
wasn't going to play nice!

At that moment, Sparrow hurried
by and stepped on Duchess's worksheet
for Home Evilnomics. I knew if
someone didn't pick up her papers soon,
they'd all be trampled. I bent over to
pick them up and—

I was yanked upward.

Faybelle had grabbed the bow on the
back of my apron.

"Sorry, Duchess, but you'll have
to clean up the papers _you_ dropped.
Our merry crew has detention, and
our cleaning hexpertise is needed in the
Grimmnasium." Faybelle took one of
my hands and Lizzie took the other.

Before I could say fiddledeedee, they led me away from a fairy shocked Duchess.

You can imagine how confused I was. Faybelle stood up to Duchess for me! And Lizzie and Kitty did, too.

I stopped in front of the doors to the Grimmnasium and thanked them.

But something was bothering me. Why were they suddenly being nice?

Then came Surprise #4: They said they've always liked me. Even Faybelle, who I wasn't sure actually liked anyone. But it turns out that Faybelle likes me just fine, and she even told me that she respects the way I stick to my story. She said she thinks I will make a fine Snow White someday.

Now <u>there's</u> something I never imagined would happen today—that I'd receive a fairy nice compliment from Faybelle!

What a topsy-turvy day this has been!

Charm you later!
Apple White

Chapter 6

O h hex!" Apple took in the Grimmnasium disaster zone. "How can such cute little creatures do such major damage?"

Apple was nervous about getting things cleaned up in enough time to persuade Headmaster Grimm to reinstate the dance. The destroyed decorations looked even worse than she'd remembered. She regretted sending the woodland creatures outside to gather berries and nap in the shade.

"Don't worry, Apple. We can fix this quick as a game of croquet." Lizzie surveyed the room.

"*Purr*fectly," agreed Kitty.

"Really?" Apple couldn't hide her surprise. "You'll all help?"

Faybelle nodded. "We want the dance, too. I want to wear my ice-blue gown with the black velvet trim, and the cheerhexers choreographed a dance to teach everyone. So...what now?"

Apple realized that they were waiting for her to assign jobs. They were all going to work together! She hadn't lost her leadership skills ever after all.

"Just know I don't do water. No sponges or mops for me," declared Kitty. "Or apple-bobbing bins."

"We should each do what we're good at." Apple handed Kitty the knotted strands of twinkling lights to untangle.

Faybelle flew to the ceiling and unhooked bits of crumpled garlands.

Lizzie stood back and shouted orders to everyone...but at least they were helpful orders.

Apple tried her best to repair the decorations. She fashioned new flowers from ripped tissue paper, but the wilting petals looked as if they'd suffered the Evil Queen's icy glare.

"Those are sad," Faybelle agreed.

"How can I ever re-create the Enchanted Forest with what's left? All I have are felt leaves with tiny bite marks and chewed-up apple cores. Recycling and repurposing will only go so far." Apple threw up her arms in defeat.

"So change the theme," said Faybelle.

Change the theme? Apple's theme was hexcellent. And it had won the committee vote.

Apple shook her head. "The Enchanted Forest theme is fairy important."

"Really?" Faybelle shrugged. "Some muse-ic, friends, and fun are all I need."

"I need a nap," called Kitty.

"Oh cards!" cried Lizzie.

Kitty followed Lizzie's orders to get straight to work and batted the cracked chocolate eggs into a basket. Lizzie joined in with her croquet mallet.

"Time for tunes." Faybelle switched on her MirrorPhone. Tailor Quick's voice filled the Grimmnasium. Each girl took a turn singing lead, pretending the brooms and mops were microphones.

Apple realized she was having more fun

than she'd had last night when the committee had decorated for the first time. This
was what the dance was all about: having
fun with friends. If only Duchess could see
that.

Wait a spell! Apple thought.

"Faybelle, you just gave me a great idea for
a new theme," she declared over the muse-ic.

"Oh yeah?" said Faybelle.

"The theme is *fun*," Apple said simply.
"We've cleaned the floors, the walls, and the
tables. We'll hang lights and streamers and let
the students bring the fun. It's fairy simple."

Faybelle's face broke out into a wide grin.

"I like it!" declared Lizzie.

"You like what?" asked Raven. She, Briar, and
Maddie had just pushed open the Grimmnasium door. "Wow! We came to help you, but it
looks spelltacular in here."

"This already feels like a party!" Maddie began to dance to the muse-ic.

"We're having some fun while we work," Apple hexplained.

"We?" Raven's eyes darted between Apple and Faybelle. "Really?"

Apple nodded.

"We brought you food, Apple. We know you missed lunch, too." Briar pulled out a slightly smushed princess pea-butter sandwich.

"I got you a fritter." Maddie produced an apple fritter from under the turquoise silk top hat on her head. Then she reached under the hat again. "Two fritters. Three fritters. Four fritters. Well, I say. They just go on and on and on and on...."

Maddie stopped reaching under her hat. She placed it on her mint-green-and-lavender hair. "The End," she declared.

"Yum!" Apple realized how hungry she was. "Lizzie, Kitty, Faybelle, let's eat!"

As she shared the delicious food, she saw Briar share a perplexed look with Raven.

"Apple, can we talk to you?" asked Briar.

"Of course." Apple swallowed her mouthful of pea-butter sandwich.

"Privately."

"Oh." Apple didn't like to leave others out.

She gave an apologetic wave to Lizzie, Kitty, and Faybelle, who were sipping the elderberry tea that Maddie poured from a flowered teapot. Then she stepped to the side with Briar and Raven.

"Why are you singing and laughing with Faybelle?" whispered Briar. "Raven told me what she did to you."

"This mess isn't really only her fault," said Apple.

"Maybe, but she blamed you. Has she apologized?" Raven asked.

"Well, no . . ." Apple thought about Faybelle putting Duchess in her place. "Maybe she did in her own way. I know she has good hidden underneath all her Dark Fairy badness."

Raven smiled. "You always find the good in everyone."

Apple was touched that her friends were looking out for her. "They just want what we all want—to get the dance back."

"Do you think that will happen?" asked Raven.

"I hope so." Apple took a deep breath. "I'm going to talk to Headmaster Grimm right now. Wish me luck."

Diary Entry

Oh my fairy godmother, Diary. I can't believe what just happened. It was a totally spelltacular fairy-fail.

Really, there's no other word for it. He totally shut the book on me.

I was feeling so determined when I went to find him. I gave him my most impassioned speech about why I felt the dance should be back on. I poured out my heart.

And he liked it. He really did.

He inspected the Grimmnasium and was royally impressed. While I was gone, Faybelle had hung cheerhexing pom-poms from the ceiling. Kitty had turned on the little twinkling lights (then quickly disappeared into the shadows), and Lizzie had built a big chocolate fountain out of playing cards!

Next we went to check out the Castleteria. I was feeling super hopeful at this point. I was already planning my outfit for tonight. Basically, Diary, I was counting my beans before the beanstalk had grown.

You get the idea.

Because as soon as we all entered the Castleteria, Headmaster Grimm frowned and said, "I see you had some help, Ms. White."

I froze. And then I saw them.

Two rabbits had come back all on their own to shine the silver goblets and tureens. Weren't they the sweetest honey-bunnies to do hextra cleaning?

Headmaster Grimm saw what they were doing and quickly realized that we had broken one of his rules. Make that, I had broken one of his rules. I made sure to tell him that, too—I was the one who brought in the helpers, and the other girls had not been involved.

Headmaster Grimm asked the girls if it was true. They hesitated—I could tell they didn't want me to take all the blame. But I deserved it.

"Go on, tell the truth," I said, and smiled at my new friends.

And they did. I was proud of them. Just this morning, Faybelle lied fairy easily to Headmaster Grimm. And now, maybe with a little help from my positive influence, she told the truth!

Headmaster Grimm thought for a few minutes in silence. Then he told us that the dance was back on!

But as punishment for breaking his rule about not having any help with the cleanup, I was forbidden to attend.

Faybelle and Lizzie were about to speak up for me when Sparrow rushed in. The Potions class had mixed fizzy ginger root with porcupine quills instead of walrus whiskers. Cauldrons were bubbling over, sending rivers of purple foam through the basement.

Headmaster Grimm hurried to the door, grumbling about how first-years never learn and wondering where to find goblin toenail clippings to reverse the reaction.

Faybelle called after him, asking him to please reconsider and let me go to the dance. It was so fairy sweet of her to try to help me! But it was all for nothing. He said that I cannot set foot in the Grimmnasium tonight. "And that's The End of that."

Can you believe it? Neither can I.

But at least the dance is back on for everyone else!

Charm you later,
Apple White

Chapter 7

Raven Queen checked her thronework for the third time, hoping to find a mistake. She erased the *8* and rewrote it, making the circles as round as she could. She chewed the end of her quill, then tapped it on her desk. What else could she fix?

"I know what you're doing." Apple sat at her vanity and brushed her shiny hair. She gave it seven hundred strokes every night to keep it bouncy.

"What am I doing?" Raven looked up.

"You're pretending that you have tons of thronework so you can delay getting dressed. You don't want me to feel sad when I see you get ready for the dance."

Raven bit her lip. "Don't you? Feel sad, I mean."

"I do." Apple turned. "But it will make me sadder if you go to the dance wearing *that*."

Raven looked down at her violet tunic, black leggings, and fuzzy lavender socks and smirked. "It can be a protest outfit. To let the teachers know I stand with you."

"I made a mistake, and it's only fair that I take my punishment like a princess. I don't want you to protest." Apple stood and flung open Raven's closet. "I want you to go to the dance and have double fun—for you and for me. You must look fableous times two."

It felt so fairy wrong to Raven to be getting

ready to go to the dance without Apple. Dressing together was as much fun as going to the party. They'd turn on muse-ic and help each other pick outfits. Neither would walk out the door without the Royal Roomie Seal of Approval.

Tonight would be the first time they hadn't done that together.

"I like this one." Apple held up a dark-purple dress with a fitted black bodice covered in black rhinestones. The skirt was constructed of layers of black and dark-purple tulle with an overlay of delicate black lace.

"Me too." Raven fidgeted, suddenly unsure how to act with her friend. "I can go get dressed in Maddie's room so you don't have to watch."

"And ruin the little fun I get tonight? Have you flipped your crown?" cried Apple. "Helping you makes me feel like I'm going, too."

Raven was amazed at Apple's good spirits. Raven didn't think she could be so upbeat if the glass slipper were on the other foot. She decided to let Apple make her fashion choices. "Okay, then, what shoes should I choose?"

Apple picked out plum suede platforms with thin ribbons that tied at the ankles. She fastened a choker that held a silver teardrop pendant around Raven's neck. Raven let Apple spin the tunes—Katy Fairy, of course. Then Apple styled Raven's long hair half up, half down with soft curls. Raven drew the line at Apple's choice of a sweet apple blossom headband. Instead, she rested a spiky, silver tiara on her dark hair. A princess had to stay true to herself.

"Hello and good-bye!" Maddie entered the room, out of breath because she was hopping. Backward. "Is everyone hexcited about the dance? I usually wear pants to a dance, but tonight I'm wearing a hat. Do you have a fork I can borrow to match my not-pants?" Briar followed.

"Oh, I adore your dresses!" Apple clapped her approval.

"Thank you." Briar blushed. "I feel terrible leaving you behind, Apple. Isn't there anything we can do?"

"The merry-go-round is in motion." Maddie spun on her heels. "There's no pulling the horse from the carriage now."

"Maddie's right. I can't undo what's done. I want you to have fun and then come back and tell me *everything*." Apple smiled at her best friends forever after. "Come on. No gloomy ogre faces."

Maddie scrunched her face, working hard to mimic a growling ogre. Briar and Apple laughed, but Raven was too busy reading something on her MirrorPhone to look up.

Briar and Apple started pulling silly ogre faces of their own, but Apple stopped when she noticed Raven tilting her screen toward Maddie. Maddie nodded and nudged Briar. Briar peeked at it, and her eyes widened.

"What's up?" asked Apple, moving closer for a look.

"It's just a hext." Raven tucked her Mirror-Phone into her black velvet purse with the silver chain. "We're going to go now, okay?"

"Okay, sure. But...who hexted you?" asked Apple, curious.

"Uh, no one. The person had the wrong number. Happens all the time, right? Spell you later." Raven made for the door. Maddie and Briar hurried after her, all in a sudden rush to leave, acting as if the clock had struck midnight and their dresses were going to turn into rags.

Apple watched them glide down the hall toward the Grimmnasium. She smiled and waved.

It was not until she'd closed the door and was all alone in her room that she let her smile fade.

Diary Entry

We did it, Diary! At this fairy moment, the entire school is at the dance—the same dance that was canceled just this morning. I'm so happy all our hard work paid off.

But I have to admit...I can't help being a little sad, too. I really, really wanted to go to the dance. And sitting on my bed all by myself is lonely.

Even though it's just you and me tonight, Diary, I'm trying to make the fairy best of it.

I put on my favorite old flannel pj's that I always keep in the back of my drawer. They have a red-and-green smiley-face apple pattern that's too nursery-rhyme school to wear in front of my friends. I haven't worn them in forever after, but they are super soft and I love snuggling up in them.

They are the most royally perfect outfit for a night in by myself.

Hmmm...

Diary, it feels fairy strange to be all alone. I'm almost _never_ alone at Ever After High. If I'm not in my room with Raven, I'm in class or the Castleteria or doing an activity with one of my friends. Anywhere I go, a friendly face waits to say "Once upon a hi."

Hexcept now.

It's certainly quiet in here without Raven, Briar, and Maddie.

Most especially Maddie!

I know, I know, Diary. I need to focus on the positive. Even though I'm on my own tonight and I'm sad to be missing the dance, I got the dance back for all my friends, and that was fairy important. When I picture them dancing under the twinkly lights, that fresh-out-of-the-oven apple cobbler feeling warms me up.

I just have to keep thinking about the happy part and not about being alone and missing out on the fun. As Maddie said, that story has already been written, printed, and put on the shelves. Time to move the plot forward.

That makes perfect sense to me.

What I don't understand is, what was up with my friends just before they left? Raven hadn't wanted me to see something. But what? And what caused them to leave so fast?

Best friends forever after shouldn't keep secrets.

Unless they were keeping a secret to protect me. Maybe that hext was mean and would've upset me. I have had enough bad news and tears for one day, that's for sure.

It's time to focus on the next chapter. I'm going to put down my quill and close my eyes and picture tomorrow.

I'll go right to breakfast. There will be no mice or cleaning or

Chapter 8

Apple White had fallen asleep.

She dreamed she was dancing in the meadow. Pastel flowers opened their petals in celebration. Butterflies fluttered in a wave of golden color. White mice circled her, singing and feeding her bits of orange cheese. Then a rabbit appeared and waved her toward the Enchanted Forest with its big, floppy ear.

Apple and the little mice followed it, prancing through the tall grass. They walked and hiked and ran. But they couldn't get there. The Enchanted Forest looked so close, but it was so far, far away. Apple called for help.

No one was there. The rabbit had gone. The mice had gone. Her friends had gone.

She was all by herself.

Then she heard a *chirp, chirp, chirp*.

A bluebird! She searched the cloudless sky, then the trees, for the bluebird.

Chirp, chirp, chirp.

The bluebird called to her again.

Where was it? Why wouldn't it show itself?

Apple's heart beat faster as she whirled around, searching.

Chirp, chirp—

The sound was next to her head.

Apple opened her eyes. She blinked, unsure where she was. It took her a moment to realize that she wasn't in a meadow. She was in her room at Ever After High.

Chirp, chirp, chirp.

The bluebird's call startled her.

She looked around, still a bit fuzzy from her unintended sleep. Had it flown in from the window? Apple pushed back the white eyelet curtains. Moonlight bathed the room in a pale glow, but the window was firmly shut. There couldn't be a bird in the room.

Apple shook her head to clear it. She pushed aside her diary, which was wedged under her arm, fished her quill out from under the fluffy comforter, and sat up.

Chirp, chirp, chirp.

Suddenly, Apple realized the chirping sound was coming from her MirrorPhone. It was the special tone she'd set for her incoming hexts. She reached over to her bedside table and glanced at the screen.

FAYBELLE: meet me @ mice closet

Apple considered this. Why in ever after did Faybelle want her to go back there? Fairy, fairy strange.

Then she noticed she'd slept through a bunch of other hexts. She scrolled to read them.

LIZZIE: r u coming?

FAYBELLE: did u get my hext????? mice closet, k?

RAVEN: storage closet by Castleteria— Royally Important. 👑

FAYBELLE: hello? u there?

KITTY: where r u?????

LIZZIE: Answer us! Or off with your head!

RAVEN: need u @ storage closet!

FAYBELLE: all teachers r in the
Grimmnasium/sneak out—now

LIZZIE: ???

RAVEN: Royal Roomie Request!

Apple scrambled off her bed. "Royal Roomie Request" was their new secret code to let the other know that they needed the other right away. It meant hocus focus! No diddle-dawdling allowed.

What was wrong? Apple started to hext Raven back, then stopped.

Her friend needed her—and that was all she needed to know.

Apple raced out the door, not bothering to change her clothes or throw a robe over her silly pj's. Her bare feet padded down the empty halls. Apple kept her eyes peeled for roaming teachers in search of any wayward students. Faybelle had been right. She had the halls to herself.

Apple spotted the storage closet. It was funny that she'd never noticed it before, yet today she'd been here twice. The first time hadn't brought a happy ending. She hoped this visit wouldn't send her to Headmaster Grimm's office again.

Checking the deserted halls one last time, Apple reached for the doorknob. Her hand shook slightly. She paused and listened, hexpecting to hear the *squeak* of the mice. Or the chatter of her friends.

Silence greeted her.

She swallowed hard, trying to calm her nerves. Why did Raven, Faybelle, Kitty, and Lizzie need her so desperately? What was waiting on the other side?

Chirp, chirp, chirp.

Apple jumped at the sound. She quickly pulled her MirrorPhone from her pajama pocket and pressed MUTE, hoping it hadn't alerted any teachers. She read the new hext.

> RAVEN: r u ok???? worried bc you're
> not hexting back

How topsy-turvy, thought Apple. *I'm worried about her and now she's worried about me!*

> APPLE: I'm here.

Then she tucked her MirrorPhone into her pocket, turned the knob, and pulled open the door.

The closet was dark. Apple blinked, unable to see anything.

"Raven?" she called in a loud whisper.

No answer.

Apple took a tentative step inside, her bare toes cold on the stone floor. Her fingers fumbled to find the light switch. Suddenly, brightness flooded the room and—

"*Surprise!*"

Apple nearly tumbled backward in shock.

Oh my fairy godmother!

She was no longer in the storage closet. She was standing in the most magnificent ballroom ever after! And her friends were there, clapping and cheering.

"Where in Ever After are we?" Apple felt as if she'd detoured into the wrong story. "What happened to the closet?"

Farrah stepped forward. She wore a beautiful pale-blue gown encrusted with tiny crystals, and her silver wings poked out the back. "The closet was too small and too drab, so I enchanted it. I was going for elegant. Do you like the ballroom?"

Apple spun about, taking in the glamour. A cascading staircase led into an enormous pale-pink-and-gold ballroom. Twelve crystal chandeliers hung from the ceiling, sending dapples of light onto one of the largest dance floors she had ever seen. Chiffon drapes covered the walls, and gold tables with glowing tea lights bordered the room. The tables and chairs had been made out of playing cards, and Apple knew that was the work of Lizzie.

"I love it!" Apple turned back to Farrah. "But why did you do it? What's this party for?"

"It's for you." Faybelle stepped up. She wore her ice-blue dress with the black velvet trim.

"Me?" Apple still couldn't piece the plot together.

Raven jostled her way forward. A big smile covered her face. "Don't you hear everyone cheering? Everyone wanted to celebrate what a good friend you are."

Apple suddenly did hear it. Her friends were clapping and saying her name. She took in the happy faces that surrounded her—Briar; Maddie; Lizzie; Kitty; Hunter; Daring, Dexter, and Darling Charming; and so many others.

Melody Piper was out on the dance floor DJing. The Three Blind Mice led Kitty, Jillian Beanstalk, and Cedar in a line dance. Ginger Breadhouse and Rosabella sipped tall, frosty milk-and-cookies shakes. Ashlynn sat at a table and tapped her toe to the beat, afraid she'd lose a shoe if she kicked up her heels. Blondie circled the room, filming the action.

It felt as if the whole school were there.

"Wait. What about the dance in the Grimm-nasium?"

"That's still happening, but how could we enjoy it without you?" said Raven.

"You worked so hard to bring back the dance, so we decided to bring a secret dance to you," finished Faybelle.

"You two?" Apple looked back and forth between Raven and Faybelle. They weren't known for getting along. In fact, last month Mr. Badwolf had ended up assigning them different partners when they couldn't complete a General Villainy project together.

"It was Faybelle's idea," Raven said with a smile.

Faybelle threaded her arm through Apple's. "I owe you an apology. It was wrong of me to pretend that you were part of our prank. I'm actually surprised that Headmaster Grimm believed me—I'm not hexactly known for my trustworthiness. But I should have told him the truth."

"Thanks." Apple gave a sweet-as-pie smile. It was nice to hear the apology spoken out loud.

"But you know what? I'm glad I didn't tell the truth," said Faybelle.

Raven groaned. "Oh for fairy's sake! What kind of apology is *that*?"

"Relax, Raven. What I meant was, I got to know Apple today. I saw how much she cares about everyone, not just her friends. She put our happiness before her own—mine, too, and I wasn't even nice to her. And she's fun. Who knew?"

"I knew," said Raven.

"Me too," said Briar.

"Me seven," added Maddie.

"Count off!" cried Lizzie. "Me nineteen!"

"Me, um...twenty? Or should I say five?" said Rosabella.

Apple wasn't sure what was more incredible—this enchanted ballroom in the storage closet, or the fact that Faybelle and Raven had cooked it up together for her. "Thank you, everyone."

"The spell ends at midnight, and the ballroom turns back into a storage closet," Farrah informed everyone. "So let's get this party started!"

Melody Piper turned up the muse-ic's volume. Farrah's spell had soundproofed the ballroom, so their secret was safe.

Apple twirled on the crowded dance floor.

She had never-ever-after thought she'd be dancing in an enchanted storage closet surrounded by friends new and old.

Then the closet door banged open, loud enough to be heard over the pumping bass of the muse-ic. Duchess stood in the doorway with her arms folded and let out a disapproving honk. "Whatever-after is going on in here?"

Melody turned down the volume.

The Three Blind Mice stopped their routine mid–slide-to-the-left.

All eyes turned to Duchess.

"I am royally honked off that you are all in a closet instead of in the Grimmnasium. How dare you have a party and not invite me!" She ruffled her feathers. "I demand to know what this party is about."

"This is a party that Apple can come to," Raven hexplained.

"We created it so she could be included, too," said Faybelle.

"You're all at this party just for *Apple*?" Duchess appeared both surprised and hurt. "But look at her! She's in pajamas and bare feet. She isn't wearing a party dress. At the dance in the Grimmnasium, everyone looks spelltacular. She didn't even care enough to get dressed!"

Apple gazed down at her childish pajamas and felt a blush creep up her neck. She hadn't even realized she was still wearing them. She'd spent hours searching for the most perfect party outfit and now she was dancing in old sleepwear! What would everyone think?

Her bottom lip trembled as she waited for the laughter.

It never came. No one seemed to care what she wore—hexcept Duchess.

"Frou-frou-whoop-dee-do dresses and décor don't make a party, Duchess," Maddie pointed out. "Fun absotootly comes from friends. And radishes."

"We don't care about the clothes on the outside, we care about the person on the inside," added Raven.

"And Apple is fairy wonderlandiful on the inside!" Kitty declared.

"Well, if that's the way it is." Duchess arched her neck and began to glide away.

"Don't fly off just yet." Farrah touched Duchess's shoulder.

Duchess looked around. She had to admit that this enchanted ballroom-in-a-closet party was rocking. Everyone had their hands in the air as Melody blasted the beat.

Duchess felt her feathers flutter and her toes point. She couldn't help it. She wanted to dance, too. She gulped, swallowing her pride.

"Can I join the party?" she asked Faybelle in a small voice.

"If it were up to me, I'd tell you to fly the coop. You've been really wicked to Apple," Faybelle pointed out.

"I say, off with your feathered head!" cried Lizzie.

"But lucky for you, it's not my choice—or Lizzie's," said Faybelle.

"Hrrumph!" Lizzie stomped her foot.

"Who is it up to?" asked Duchess.

"It's up to Apple."

Everyone waited quietly to hear what Apple would say.

Diary Entry

The.

Best.

Time.

Ever - After!!!!!!!!

I'm back in my room and cozy under my covers. I didn't even have to get changed to go to bed—a definite perk to wearing pj's to a surprise dance. Maybe our next school

dance should be a pajama party! What
do you think?

Raven is already asleep, but I'm still
too hexcited to close my eyes. The dance
was truly something out of a fairytale.

Okay, I know, I know...you want
to know what I said to Duchess.

What do you think I said?

The more the merrier, of course!

I do not believe in hexcluding anyone.

I opened the door wide and let in
Duchess and her friends.

Then I went back to the dance
floor. Melody had started a freeze
dance game. When Melody stopped the
muse-ic, we each had to freeze in place.
If you moved, you were out. Cedar

was by far the best at it. She stood as still as a plank of wood every single time!

And soon enough, it was time for a thronecake break. All that dancing can work up an appetite!

I'd gone to the dessert table when I noticed Duchess standing by herself in a corner.

I realized everyone was sitting in pairs or groups. No one had invited her to join them.

So I invited her to sit with me, and we shared my thronecakes. Turns out, Duchess really shows her soft side when you share your dessert. She was surprised I was being nice to her after everything that had happened that day.

I told her that being nice is actually really easy—plus, it makes you feel good. And then Duchess apologized to me!

Wow!

Duchess hexplained that she's always wanted to be as popular as she thinks I am. She wanted to be Top Princess.

I told her there's no Top Princess at Ever After High. No one is higher or better or more important than anyone else.

But Duchess said that sometimes it doesn't feel like that's true.

Then she told me something that really opened my eyes as to why she's not so nice most of the time. She said she wished she had a more popular fairytale...and a Happily Ever After. She told me that sometimes she gets really jealous and frustrated that I am practically guaranteed a Happily Ever After, and that she has no way of ever finding one for herself.

Can you imagine what that must feel like, Diary? I can, and it feels TERRIBLE.

Good leaders put themselves in the shoes of others. (Not literally, of course!) When I thought about it, I realized how it could seem really unfair to Duchess to be stuck with a story that doesn't have a Happily Ever After when so many of us here at Ever After High have that to look forward to. No wonder she's so grumpy all the time.

But then I reminded Duchess of just how special her story is. She can turn into a beautiful swan whenever she'd like. Not to mention, she's one of the fairy best dancers in the whole school, and I bet one day she'll be one of the best in all of Ever After. She's talented and unique. That's just as important as having a fairytale Happily Ever After.

So I dragged Duchess out to the dance floor to show off just how talented she is. And, oh my fairy godmother, could she dance! We were having the time of our storybook lives when we heard—knock, knock.

You know how this story goes by now, right?

Every time I've opened that closet door today, something <u>MAJOR</u> has happened. I didn't need my house blown down three times to get the message. I was <u>NOT</u> opening that door by myself.

I gathered Raven, Maddie, Faybelle, Lizzie, Kitty, and Duchess around me.

<u>Knock, knock.</u>

The door opened, and there stood Headmaster Grimm. His forehead creased as he surveyed the enchanted ballroom.

My stomach dropped. For the third time today, I was going to get in trouble! Me, Apple White! What was the kingdom coming to?

But you know what? Headmaster Grimm didn't stop our party. He liked

that everyone had put friendship first. He
was impressed we'd worked together and
were getting along, even with no teachers
on hand to keep the peace. He invited the
students in the Grimmnasium to join us
in the closet, and we all danced until the
clock was ready to strike twelve.

Don't get me wrong. He still gave out
a punishment for breaking the rules. I
mean, he is the headmaster after all. This
time it wasn't cleaning. He took dessert
away for a whole week. No thronecakes
or plum pudding or apple dumplings.

But it wasn't only _my_ dessert
that went _poof_! Everyone's treats
disappeared. We were all in this one
together. And that was sweet enough to
make up for the lost sweets.

Night-night, Diary.

This mixed-up, moused-up, cleaned-up, magic-closet day turned out to be even more fableous than I'd ever after imagined.

I can't wait to see what tomorrow will bring!

Charm you later!
Apple White

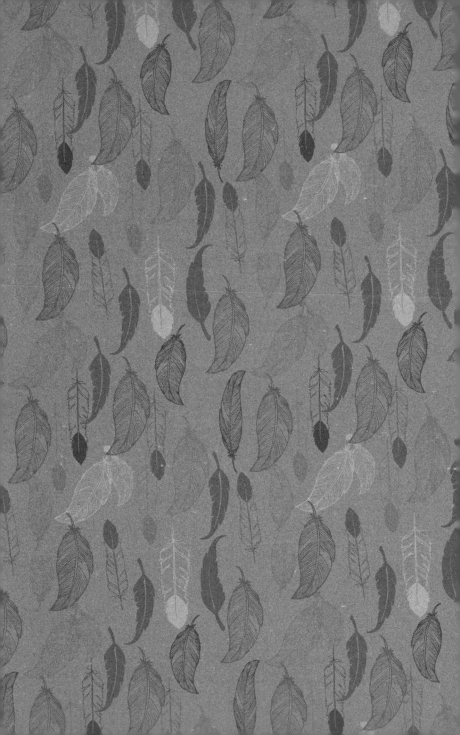

Did you ♥ reading

Apple White's diary?

Then you'll love

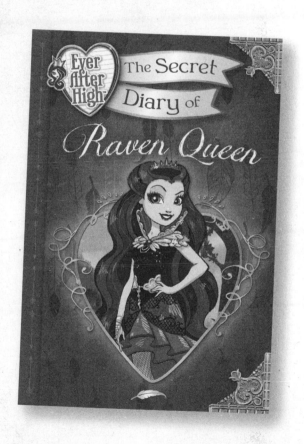

Turn the page for a sneak peak!

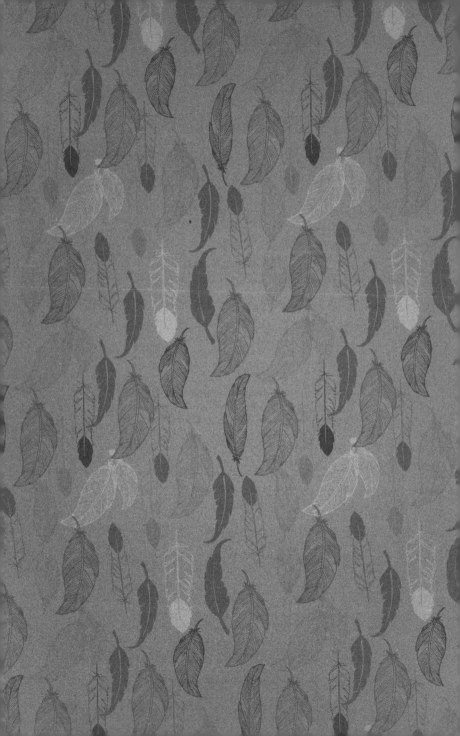

Diary Entry

I don't know how this diary-writing thing is supposed to work. I've never kept a diary before. I royally hope I'm doing it right. Apple White seems to love writing in hers. Every night, Apple sits cross-legged on her bed in our room at Ever After High and scribbles happy thoughts in her diary. (Wait a spell. Apple would <u>never</u> scribble. She has beautiful handwriting. Me, not so much,

but I'm working on that. Is this legible?)
I always wonder what she's writing, but
whenever I ask, she just gives me a smile
and says, "Diaries are secret, Raven!" I
know she's right, but I can't help but feel
just a little bit curious! Apple says writing
her thoughts down lets her make sense of
her story. But every time I try to rewrite my
story, everything goes _so_ wrong. And that's
why I'm trying this diary thing—maybe
it will help me make sense of my story,
what-ever-after that may be.

    This is how it all started, Diary....

    Yesterday, Baba Yaga assigned our
Magicology class homework to do over
Spring Break. Our assignment is to write
down all the spells we do, and when we get
back to Ever After High, we'll look at the

results and learn how to make the spells better or stronger. Baba Yaga floated down the aisles of our classroom on her magic pillow, passing out diaries to the rest of the class, but when she got to me, she dropped <u>two</u> journals on my desk. Everyone else got <u>one</u> journal.

Assuming she'd made a mistake, I told Baba Yaga that she had given me two journals. I tried to give one back, but she just stared at me. "You're going home today, aren't you, Miss Queen? As the daughter of the Evil Queen, I hope that you will do <u>so many</u> evil spells this Spring Break that you will easily fill two journals."

Two journals? <u>Hex no!</u> I won't fill even one journal. I will <u>not</u> be doing that many spells over Spring Break, and definitely no evil spells! I'd like to cast no spells at all, but I'll have to do some so I don't fail my assignment. What I really want to do over the break is have a fairy relaxing time. But I couldn't say that to Baba Yaga. She definitely wouldn't want to hear about those plans.

My BFFAs and I have been looking forward to this break forever after. I'm so used to talking to my best friends every day here at Ever After High that it will be a little weird to not have someone to share all my thoughts and ideas with. That's when I got a fableous idea. I'd turn the second journal into a diary! I can "talk" to you, Diary, and share all my thoughts and experiences. You'll understand what it's like to be the daughter of the Evil Queen—to be the girl who refuses to be evil and wants to write her own ever after.

At least, I hope you'll get it.

Spring Break starts after lunch today. Some of my friends are going home together. Briar Beauty is going home with Apple White. Rosabella Beauty is going home with Darling Charming. Cerise Hood invited me and Madeline Hatter to her house in the Dark Forest. That was an invitation I was fairy hexcited about. I feel lucky every day that I have such great BFFAs. When I was a little kid, I didn't really have that many friends, and I didn't have many sleepovers. Okay, I had <u>zero</u>. A lot of families don't want the daughter of the Evil Queen sleeping over at their houses. It's hard sometimes, but not everyone believes that I'm not like my mom. I understand it—I mean, my mom is a _legend_ in Ever After and she's done some seriously wicked things, and I'm supposed to be just like her. But I'm not, and maybe one day all of Ever After will realize that. So the fact that Cerise's family wanted me to visit feels good. Her family isn't like other families. Everyone knows her mom is Red Riding Hood, but no one would ever guess that her dad is...Mr. Badwolf. (_Shhh_, Diary, that's a big secret! I can tell you because that's just like telling myself...but I would never-ever-after tell anyone else that.) Cerise's parents totally flipped the script!

Maddie said yes to the invitation right away. (Actually, what she said was "Do bees kneel at tea parties? Abso-TEA-lutely!"

But that means "I'm in!" in Riddlish.) I definitely wanted to say yes, too. It would be hexcellent to stay up all night talking with Maddie and Cerise. Plus, Cerise's mom bakes the most delicious pies and cakes, and Cerise said we'd go on a picnic in the woods…but then I thought of home. I miss Cook and her twins, Butternut and Pie. I haven't seen my father, the Good King, in forever after. I want to tell him about all the fableous things I've been up to at school. This was a tough choice.

Go home or visit Cerise and her family?

Then I got a hext message. My dad invited me to sit next to him in the royal box for the Gallant Princes on White Horses race. The race is a big deal. All the king's horses and all the king's men go.

Princesses and fairies get dressed up and wear the most enchanting hats. Dad rides his horse around the track before the race starts. He invited me to ride next to him. He's never asked me to do that before, but he says I'm old enough now, and that he wants his spelltacular daughter by his side for all the kingdom to see.

That does it! Decision made. I'm going home for Spring Break for some overdue dad-daughter time.

Spell you later,
Raven

Chapter 1

Faybelle Thorn stood in front of the heavy door leading to the tower attic and peered down the empty hallway again. Was she alone? She had to be triple sure. It was against the rules for students to go up in the attic. If she were caught, Headmaster Grimm would probably give her detention again, and she'd spent enough time there already this year.

I won't get caught, she decided.

Faybelle hesitated for a moment. After the last time she'd sneaked up there, she'd pinkie-promised herself that she'd never-ever-after go again. But Dark Fairies are known to break promises. Even promises they make to themselves.

Faybelle recited a fairy spell, and the heavy chains crisscrossing the door immediately turned as bendy as gummy dragons. She pushed them aside and opened the door.

Faybelle's skin prickled as she ran up the narrow spiral staircase. Enchanting the door and being inside the dusty tower attic wouldn't get her into *that* much trouble. But what she was doing in the attic would—talking to *Her*. Even her mom, the Dark Fairy who'd cursed Sleeping Beauty to slumber for one hundred years, wouldn't approve. Faybelle didn't want her mom to be angry, but she couldn't help herself. Visiting with the Evil Queen made her feel brave and special. She was the

Villain Club president and already Ever After High's Fairy-to-Fear, but if the students knew that she was talking to *Her*, they'd be royally petrified.

Just thinking about all that fear made the tips of her wings tingle.

But no one could know. Ever.

Faybelle was wicked, but she wasn't stupid. The Evil Queen was locked up in mirror prison and hidden away in the attic for fairy good reason. She'd rampaged Wonderland, and then that one time she destroyed Ever After High when Dragonsport was brought back to the school…with Faybelle's help. But Faybelle really learned her lesson that time. The Evil Queen's out-of-control evil was dangerously off-book. Even Faybelle knew she needed to stay inside the mirror from now on. But it couldn't hurt to just talk to her.…

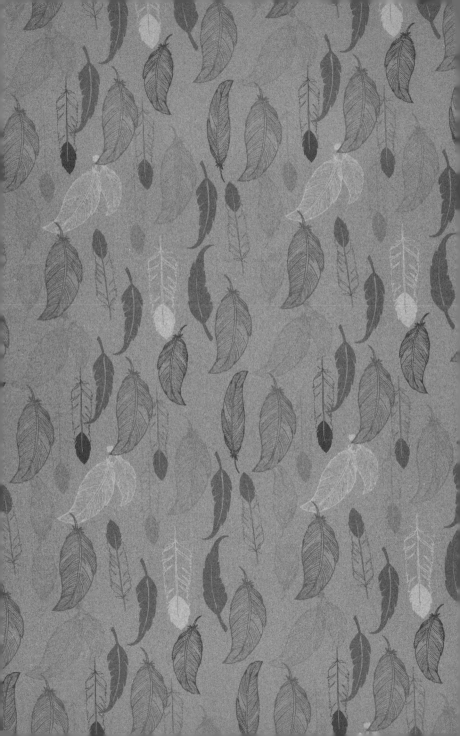